EEK! A Dinosaur!

Written by Keri Parker

Illustrated by Suhad Khayo

Formatted by

Lemon House Publishing

For Mom and Dad, who always supported me and all my crazy aspirations.
Thank you for always encouraging me to chase my dreams. - K.P.

Pebbles the dinosaur sat upon the forest hill watching the blooming sunrise.

All alone, with no one to sit with.

Pebbles picked the daises,

splashed in the puddles,

and kicked the ground rocks.

"Everyones afraid of me!" Pebbles cried. And so today, like every day, Pebbles sat all alone.

Truly, nobody likes a dinosaur.

"Hi! I'm Pebbles!" he says to some local critters.

Herman the hermit crab scurries away under the rocks.

"You'll step on me with your giant feet!"

Sue the shrew scampers into her cave.

"Your teeth are so big and pointy! You'll eat me!"

Even Barry the bumblebee buzzed back to his hive.

"Ahh! You're a big scary monster."

Truly, nobody likes a dinosaur.

And so yet again,
Pebbles picked the daises,

splashed in the puddles,

and kicked the ground rocks.

Pebbles heard a little cry.
A small, blue lizard sat all alone under a bush.

"EEK!" the small creature yelped.

"Your a Di-Din-Dino-DINOSAUR!"

The lizard scampered further under the bush.

"It's okay little guy, I won't hurt you!"

"You-You-You won't?" the lizard said softly.

"Of course not! I'm not big and scary! I'm the most kind creature you'll ever find! But nobody gives me a chance," Pebbles sighed.

"I skip through the jungle,
I read all the books I can find,
And I make the worlds best leafy-green salad."

"I'm bigger than the other lizards!" the lizard groaned.
"I don't fit in."

"C'mon, we can go to my favorite hill together!"

"I'm Emmett," the lizard croaked.
"I'm Pebbles!"

Herman, Sue, and Barry gasped as they saw such a small creature walk through the jungle with such a big dinosaur.

"Maybe he's not so big and scary!" they all wondered.

And so Pebbles and his new friends all wandered to the top of forest hill to watch the blooming sunset.

"Now let's try that leafy-green salad I've been hearing so much about!" Emmett giggled.

Truly, somebody likes a dinosaur.